DEBBIE ALLEN
Dancing in the Wings

Pictures by KADIR NELSON

 Dial Books for Young Readers ✳ New York

Hohlin Allen
5 - 4 - 02

Published by Dial Books for Young Readers
A division of Penguin Putnam Inc.
345 Hudson Street
New York, New York 10014

Text copyright © 2000 by Red Bird Productions, Inc.
Pictures copyright © 2000 by Kadir Nelson
All rights reserved
Designed by Nancy R. Leo-Kelly
Text set in Breughel
Printed in Hong Kong on acid-free paper
9 10 8

Library of Congress Cataloging-in-Publication Data
Allen, Debbie.
Dancing in the wings/by Debbie Allen; pictures by Kadir Nelson.
p.   cm.
Summary: Sassy tries out for a summer dance festival in Washington, D.C.,
despite the other girls' taunts that she is much too tall.
ISBN 0-8037-2501-9
[1. Ballet—Fiction. 2. Self-confidence—Fiction. 3. Teasing—Fiction.]
I. Nelson, Kadir, ill. II. Title.
PZ7.A42528 Dan 2000   [E]—dc21   99-462181

*For each full-color painting, a pencil drawing was created, which was
then photocopied. Oil paints were then applied to the photocopy.*

For my daughter, Vivian, and Phylea, Ferlie,
Judith Jamison, Cynthia Gregory, and
all long-legged divas who are destined to dance

D. A.

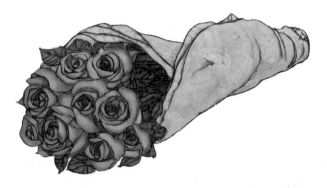

For Amel, my little "Sassy" K.N.

Ever since I was born and could see,
Everywhere I looked, I saw dance.
In the clouds as the wind blew them across the sky,
In the ripples on a pond,
Even in the sea of ants marching up and down their hills.
Dance was all around me. Dance was me.

My mom calls me Sassy, 'cause I like to put my hands on my hips and 'cause I always have something to say. Well, if you had feet as big as mine, you'd understand why.

"You should join the swimming team, since you got those long toes and don't need any fins," my older brother, Hughie, teased.

I shot right back, "At least I don't have that big forehead lookin' like a street lamp."

Mama said, "Stop all that bad talk! You act so ugly sometimes. Hughie, your big head is a sign of intelligence. And Sassy, your big feet will make your legs look longer and prettier in your ballet shoes."

My legs were longer, all right. So long that when I went to tendu, point my toe, at the bar, I tripped Miss Katherine, our teacher, who was coming down the line, looking the other way. SPLAT! She landed under the piano, her legs up in the air. *Ooo!* It was so funny. Even she had to laugh.

"Sassy!" she called out. "I'm going to tie orange bows on those big feet."

"Sorry, Miss Katherine," I answered. "But if you don't wear your glasses, you still won't see them."

One thing for sure—because of my long legs and big feet, I could jump higher and spin faster than everyone else.

I was taller than the rest of the kids at school, even the boys. At our recitals all the other girls got to dance solos and duets, and wear pretty tutus. I was too big for the boys to pick up, and too tall to be in line

with the other girls. So I watched from backstage, dancing in the wings, hoping that if I just kept dancing and trying, it would be my turn to dance in the spotlight.

One day at the end of ballet class Miss Katherine announced, "Mr. Debato from the Russian school is coming next week to look for talented young people for the summer dance festival in Washington, D.C."

The whole room turned into a whirlpool of excitement as the sign-up sheet was posted. Everyone wanted to try, especially me.

But as I wrote my name down, I heard two girls, Molly and Mona, giggle. Mona said, "Oh please, she'll never make it. They said talent, not a tyrannosaurus."

My heart seemed to stand still. For once I had nothing to say.

I couldn't hide the tears I felt welling up in my eyes, so I just grabbed my dance bag and ran to the parking lot.

I heard a familiar horn honk, and turned to see my uncle Redd in his bright green pickup truck. Uncle Redd had the whitest tight curly hair, smelled of cigars, and every day wore something red. A tie, a hat, a shirt, socks, maybe even his shoestrings, just something red. Why of all days did Mama have to send him to pick me up? Why today? I was not in the mood for his jokes or stories, but I quickly tried to dry my eyes and smile.

"I got a good one for you today, Sassy. What did the banana say to the monkey? 'Split!' Ha ha! Get it? Split, banana split." I started to cry. "Sassy, what's wrong?" he asked.

I told him what had happened. "I'm just so much taller than the other dancers, Uncle Redd."

"Sassy," he said, "you gotta look at that as a gift. Being tall means you can see all around, so you can always find the right path to take."

"No," I said, "it means I stick out like a big acne bump on someone's nose. I'll never get to dance. It's a waste of time to go to that audition."

"Listen, gal," said Uncle Redd, "if I was as tall and pretty as you, I wouldn't need to wear red so people know it's me comin' and goin'. All you gotta do to make your mark on the world is walk into a room."

By the time I got home, Uncle Redd had cheered me up, had me laughing and feeling better. As I got out of his truck, he waved good-bye, callin' out, "Make your mark, gal."

Hughie and his football friends stopped playing. Hughie yelled out, "Hey Sassy, why don't you come and play with us? We need a goalpost!"

His little mean ugly friends laughed. Boy did that make me mad!

"Sure, if we can use your big head for the ball," I shouted back. His friends screamed with laughter. Hughie got so mad, he turned red, lookin' like a tomato with that big head. Ha! We were just about to go at each other when Mama called us inside.

Late that night I lay awake, staring out my window and thinking about Uncle Redd's words. I could see myself dancing on the Milky Way, swirling like a twinkling shooting star. Next thing I knew, I was talking to myself out loud. "I'm goin' to that audition, big feet and all."

On the day of the tryout kids came from all over the city. It was so crowded. Everyone was expected to wear black, but like Uncle Redd, I picked my own color, bright yellow.

And instead of standing in the back, I squeezed between Molly and Mona, right in the front row. I ignored their snickering.

Miss Katherine came in and introduced Mr. Debato. Everyone applauded. Boy was he short! Couldn't have been more than four feet nine inches tall.

He started walking down the rows, pacing back and forth, just looking at us. Then he stopped right in front of me and said, "Young lady, why are you wearing that loud yellow leotard? I'll need to put on sunglasses to see anybody else. Please go to the back row."

Molly whispered, "See ya, wouldn't want to be ya."

"At least he noticed me!" I snapped. I put my hands on my hips and walked to the back.

The first round of the audition was center floor exercises. Mr. Debato walked around prodding and poking, making corrections. He stopped once and looked right at me but didn't say a thing. I held my breath as he dismissed almost half the kids after the first round. But not me.

Next was the adagio, the slow section. I stood as close to Mona as I could get and whispered, "Your little skinny short legs are gonna look like chicken wings next to mine."

"I'd rather look like a chicken than a turkey like you with that long neck," she answered.

"Talk to the hand," I told her. I took my leg up so high, it got stuck. Luckily I could balance on my other big foot. So I just held it until Mr. Debato remarked, "Young lady, the exercise is finished!"

"Oh!" I jumped out of position.

"Show-off," Molly grunted.

"Gobble gobble." Mona imitated a turkey.

Then came the leaps across the floor. I took off like Jackie Joyner-Kersee in the long jump at the Olympics. With one leap I sailed in the air past all the other girls. Molly and Mona watched, lookin' pea green with envy.

When I finished, Mr. Debato yelled, "Young lady, you must learn to dance *to* the music. Up on the count of one, down on the count of three! Three! Not five! You have the rhythm of a troglodyte. Again!"

I was crushed. As I passed Mona to get back in line, she said, "Next time bring your big butt down by three."

"Your mama," I said. *Ooo!* did I wish I was a wizard. I'd turn them into two big fat frogs in tutus trying to hip-hop.

By the end of the day there were only seven of us left. Mr. Debato called out everyone's name except mine and asked them to step forward.

Standing alone, I really had to fight to hold back my tears.

Then I heard him say, "Thank you all for coming today. Keep working, keep trying. You are dismissed."

Mr. Debato said to me, "Sassy, you have a great deal of potential. You have beautiful long arms and legs, but you flail about with no control. You must learn to use your feet better—and timing, timing. We have a lot of work to do when you come to Washington this summer. But please! *Please* leave that loud yellow leotard at home. All you need do to be noticed is walk into a room. Dismissed." He walked out.

Jumping and shouting, I ran to the parking lot. "I made it! I made it! Mama, I made it!"

Guess who was there to pick me up. Mama, Uncle Redd, Hughie, and half his football team piled in the back of the green truck on their way to a game. Everybody was so proud of me, even Hughie. "You go, Miss Big Foot."

"Thank you, Mr. Big Head," I said. We all laughed.

One month later Mama and I boarded the plane for Washington, D.C. She held my hand as my heart pounded when we landed.

At the school there were young dancers from Russia, Mexico, France, China, Cuba, Brazil, New York, Texas, and long-legged me from Inglewood, California.

In class the first day Mr. Debato introduced me to his twelve-year-old protégé, a boy named Dwight who was five feet ten inches tall. "Dwight, I think I have found you a partner. Meet Sassy."

Mama was right—being tall wasn't so bad after all, and neither was having a big head.

By the end of the summer Hughie had won the grand prize at space camp in Alabama, and I got to dance a duet with Dwight in the summer concert.

When Dwight lifted me high in the air, I felt like I was dancing on the Milky Way.

Me and my big feet . . . making my mark on the world.